Alfred C. Jewitt

Lays and Legends

Alfred C. Jewitt

Lays and Legends

ISBN/EAN: 9783337388331

Printed in Europe, USA, Canada, Australia, Japan

Cover: Foto ©Andreas Hilbeck / pixelio.de

More available books at **www.hansebooks.com**

LAYS AND LEGENDS.

BY

ALFRED CHARLES JEWITT.

PUBLISHED

BY AND FOR THE AUTHOR,

8, SPARSHOLT ROAD, CROUCH HILL, LONDON, N.

—

1880

LONDON :
PRINTED BY WERTHEIMER, LEA AND CO.
CIRCUS PLACE, LONDON WALL.

CONTENTS.

THE MOUNTAIN CAIRN.

In the soft silence of a summer eve
I stood alone upon the mountain's brow,
And gazed upon the scene that round me lay.
The setting sun lit up the western sky,
And in a garb of golden glory shone
The mighty hills. Before my vision lay
Moorland and meadow, woods and glittering lakes,
And fertile valleys, that stretched far away
To where on the horizon shone the sea.
Above, the evening sky beamed calm and clear,
And the light mountain breeze that fanned my cheek,
Whispered soft thoughts of peace and joy and rest.
Beside me, on the hill-top where I stood,
There rose a rugged pile of rough rude stones,
Placed thither by the hands of those who climbed,
From time to time, the mountain's massive side,
And gained his hoary summit. As I looked
Upon these records of the vanished hours,

I thought how different had been the hearts
Of those who placed them. With what varying eyes
Each traveller had looked upon the scene
That lay beneath. The young man, flushed with hope ;
The aged sage fast passing from the world;
The rich, the poor, the happy and the sad,
The great ones of the land, the peasant boy,
Perchance had each one added to the pile
Where now I stood. Then stooping to the ground,
I raised a stone that lay beside my feet,
And laid my offering upon the cairn.

So he who fain would rise from out the vale,
To the fair heights of fancy and of song,
Must tread the paths, and stand upon the ground
Trodden by many varying feet before—
The mighty, who have spoken to the earth
In glorious language ; and the weakly ones,
Who, with great hearts, have found their faltering tongues
Too feeble to give utterance to their thoughts.
Yet need he fear not. Every eye that seeks
May find new beauty in the scene; to him
Who listens to the music, on the breeze
Come voices ever old yet ever new ;

As the rough stones that made the cairn had passed
Through countless years midst fire, storm, and flood,
And taken many forms, till in the heap
No two were found alike; so is the thought,
Fashioned by joy and sorrow, calm and storm;
For God hath never made two souls alike
In everything. Therefore the humble bard,
Who loves alike the sunshine and the storm,
The shady valley and the breezy hill,
May still find subject for his lowly song,
And though with faltering steps, approach the cairn
Of life, nor fear to leave his offering there.

THE BELLS OF LIMERICK.

In days of yore, beside fair Como's lake,
There dwelt a man beloved of all his friends,
An artisan in metals, much renowned
Throughout his craft for skilful workmanship;
Who, as the crowning labour of his life—
The masterpiece of years of patient toil—
Had fashioned for a neighbouring convent tower
A chime of bells; whose soft and silvery tones
O'er land and water wafted by the breeze,
Filled the surrounding air with harmony.
When the first beam of morn with roseate hue
Lit up the eastern sky, the cadence clear
Sounded o'er waving fields of golden grain,
Through purple vineyards and green shady woods;
Awoke wild echoes high among the hills,
And softly fell on sleeping childhood's ear,
Breathing sweet dreams of melody and joy.

When the departing glory of the sun
Gilded the western heavens, and the lake
Lay one broad golden field of liquid light,
The bells' sweet voices floated o'er the flood,
Their music mingling with the evening song
Of boatmen, home returning from their toil.
On Christmas morn they rang the new-born Christ;
And when the holy Easter-tide came round,
Proclaimed in gladsome tones the risen Lord;
Their merry peal made glad the marriage feast;
And at the funeral hour, so sadly sweet
Their strains, the mourner's heart was comforted.
And he who made them, resting from his toil,
Would listen to their chiming, and his heart
Would glow with honest pride, as to his work
He with fresh vigour turned. So year by year,
Amidst the love of kindred and of friends—
His craft his mistress and his only care—
His happy life passed peacefully away.

But war broke out within that smiling land;
And the fair hills and valleys, far and wide,
Echoed the tramp of steeds and clang of arms.
A hostile band with fire and sword laid waste

The fertile country, sacked the sacred house,
And from their belfry bore the chimes away;
And the good artisan, because he dared
To raise his arm against th' invaders' power,
Was therefore banished kindred, friends, and home;
For in the code of battle might is right,
And love of country, in the conqueror's eye
Becomes a sin that calls for punishment;
So the good man was exiled from the land
He loved so well, and forced 'mid foreign scenes
To roam and labour for his daily bread.

For many weary years by land and sea
He wandered with a mournful heavy heart,
And in each town sought out the artisans
Of his own craft, and with them worked awhile,
But never tarried long in any place.
Sometimes, when lying on his lonely bed,
His thoughts would backward turn, and he would see
Once more in dreams, the vineyards and the woods,
The stately mountains, and the glittering lake,
And hear the strains of his beloved chimes,
Peaceful and soft, as in the days of old;
Then would he wake, as through his window came

The deep rich tones of a cathedral clock,
Pealing the hour; and all the varied sounds
Of a great city wakening to life.
At night-time he would wander by the sea,
And watch the billows' ceaseless ebb and flow,
Restless as his own bosom; and the clouds
Flying in haste across the moonlit sky;
Then his sad spirit longed to float away
On the eternal sea, and be at rest.
The years rolled by, and bent his form with age,
And turned his locks to snow; but stately still
His mien, as some strong fortress that has long
Withstood the tempests of the passing years,
But still stands fair in ruin, with its form
Softened and mellowed, but not spoilt by time.
One evening, as he wandered on the quay
Of an old Flemish city, and conversed
Amidst a group of sailors gathered there,
He met with one, who told him that there hung
In the cathedral tower of Limerick town
A peal of bells, of music wondrous sweet,
Brought thither from the land of Italy.
That night the old man, kneeling by his bed,
Poured forth his soul in earnest prayer to heaven,

That he once more might listen to the sound
He loved so well, then die and be at rest.

The sun was sinking low behind the hills,
And Shannon's stream lay shimmering in the light,
As the tide ebb'd away towards the sea.
Upon the banks the autumn's glorious tints,
Crimson and gold luxuriantly shone ;
And from their overhanging boughs the trees
Upon the waters cast their withered leaves.
Upon the shore the heron, still and staid,
Stood watching for his prey, while with light wing
The swallow swept the surface of the flood.
No sound disturbed the stillness, save the dip
Of oars, and the soft murmur of the stream
That rippled round a boat, that 'gainst the tide,
By four strong oarsmen rowed, made progress slow.
In the boat's stern an old man lay ; his eye
Fixed with a steadfast gaze upon the spot,
Where, 'gainst the evening sky, in dark relief
The distant city stood.   The golden sun
Sank lower in the heavens, and the tide
Had almost run its course ; but slowly still
The boat moved on.   Now nearer yet appeared

The town, where tower and bridge, and house and quay
Shone calm and peaceful in the golden light,
As towards the city, still the boat moved on.

With sudden sound, upon the evening air,
The bells rang out from the cathedral tower,
In wild sweet melody. Their silvery tones
The old man knew, and rose from where he lay,
And spread his arms aloft, as if to clasp
Some well-beloved object, while the tears
Of joy stood in his brightly beaming eye,
Then, with a soft sigh laid him down to rest.

The sun had set. The twilight shades came down,
The bright hues faded from the western sky,
The chiming ceased, and silence reigned o'er all;
Another leaf had fallen on the stream,
The spirit of the wanderer had fled,
On the fair pinions of the past upborne,
Through the bright portals of the great To-Be !

FLOWING ONWARD.

BRIGHTLY is the spring sun beaming,
In its light the river gleaming
  Swiftly flows upon its way;
Come a merry youth and maiden,
With bright smiles and laughter laden,
  Joyous in the light of day.
And he stoops, where by the flowing
Stream the fair blue flower is growing,
  Plucks it—"Love, remember me!"
And she takes the blossom, blushing,
And the river, onward rushing,
  Swiftly flows towards the sea.

Sultry hot the summer weather,
Man and wife they rest together
  From the burden of the day;
And the heart of each rejoices,
As they listen to the voices
  Of the children at their play.

High o'er head the sun is shining,
On a mossy bank reclining
  Underneath a shady tree,
Look they on the shining river,
Rolling on its course, and ever
  Flowing onward to the sea.

Autumn winds are softly sighing,
On the ground the leaves are lying,
  Twilight sheds its dying ray,
Earth and sky in shadow blending,
As an aged pair are wending
  By the stream their onward way.
In the west soft colours glowing,
O'er the scene their sweet light throwing,
  Tell of joys that used to be.
O'er the stream the wind comes sighing,
On the ground the leaves are lying,
Fast the autumn day is dying,
  And before them flows the sea.

DESERTED.

With aspect dreary, dark and chill,
Stands the old house upon the hill;
A lonely building, bleak and plain,
Built in the second George's reign.
Around its walls the light winds blow,
And sadly murmur, soft and low,
                              " Deserted."

Before its door tall poplar trees
Nod to each other in the breeze,
And seem to mock the ruined hall—
Its broken windows, crumbling wall,
Its doors fast falling to decay,
Its tottering chimney stacks—and say,
                              " Deserted."

Above the moss-grown roof doth hang
A cracked and rusted bell, whose clang
Hath long since ceased ; the turret clock
Points a past time ; the weathercock
Alone still moves upon its round,
And cries with harsh discordant sound,
               " Deserted."

Bleak desolation everywhere
Is seen. No living thing is there,
Save where upon the garden wall,
With stealthy steps a cat doth crawl ;
A wretched beast, with coat all torn,
It creeps along, alone, forlorn,
               Deserted.

In the old garden rank weeds grow,
Where yet a few fair flowerets blow ;
The columbine and marigold,
And foxgloves tall their leaves unfold ;
The rose and honeysuckle bloom,
And shed around their sweet perfume—
               Deserted.

With aspect cheerless, dark and chill,
Stands the old house upon the hill ;
Around its walls the soft winds sigh ;
But all unseen to mortal eye,
Unheard by mortal ear, a race
Of ghostly beings fill that place
                              Deserted.

They enter through the closèd doors,
And pass along the vacant floors,
The forms of those long dead and gone,
Of father, mother, daughter, son ;
The grandsire old, the blushing bride,
All gather round that fireside
                              Deserted.

Behind the hills the sun sinks low,
And casts on high his after-glow ;
Softly the evening shadows fall
Across the desolated hall,
That stands, by gloomy shade o'ercast,
Save by the spirits of the past,
                              Deserted.

SPARROWS.

THE soft light of a summer evening falls
Upon the dwelling places of the dead,
Where many a weary heart and aching head
By tender loving hands is laid to sleep.
Across the ground the twilight shadows creep,
And slowly steal athwart the chapel walls,
And upward rise, with stealthy steps to where,
Deep set within the masonry above
The portals of the holy house of prayer,
Figures the cross, the sign of faith and love.
And here the sparrows fly unto their nest,
And softly twitter as they sink to rest
Within the symbol of the Lord, who said—
" Not one of these shall fall without the Father's
     care."

ON AN OLD CLOCK.

BEFORE me now it stands
    With stationary hands,
All rusted are its wheels and worn with age :
    Its bell hath ceased to chime,
    It heeds nor tide nor time ;
No more it warns the players on life's stage.

    But in the time of old,
    Full faithfully it told
How each fleet minute winged its passing flight ;
    As on its face I gaze,
    The scenes of bye-gone days
Pass fitfully before my fancy's sight.

    I see a maiden fair,
    Upon whose brow no care
Hath se its seal, nor sorrow left its trace,

Seated at even-tide
Her window-sill beside,
Bright expectation beaming on her face;

And ever and anon
She turns her gaze upon
The time-piece by the wall, until at last
A horse's hoof is heard,
A step, a whispered word
Of love and welcome,—and the scene has passed.

For now, a miser old,
Sits counting out his gold,
As points the finger to the midnight hour;
Though wearied heart and brain,
He fondly clasps the chain
That binds him to the yellow demon's power.

Now 't is a scene of gloom;
Within a darkening room
Are met, with aching hearts and tearful eyes,
A mournful group, who stand,
A silent weeping band,
Around the bed whereon a loved one lies:

Life's sun is sinking fast,
Its day will soon be past,
Yet, ever moving o'er the dial plate,
With progress sure and slow,
Th' revolving fingers go,
Remorseless as the iron hand of fate.

The bells a merry peal
Ring out; their voices steal
Into a chamber, where a lover tried,
Marks with impatient eye
The minutes as they fly,
Till he may claim his happy, blushing bride.

With throbbing, fevered brain,
Upon his bed of pain,
The sick man, restless, tosses to and fro;
Through the long silent night
He watches for the light,
And counts the weary hours as they go.

So through the vanished years,
With all their smiles and tears,
The good old time-piece spake to one and all;

Alike to young and old,
The flight of time it told,
And marked the passing moments' rise and fall.

But all is past and gone,
Its task at last is done,
Stopped are its wheels, its bell hath ceased to chime,
With stationary hands,
Before me now it stands,
An antique image of departed time.

WAR.

April, 1878.

WAR! War! War! War!
The cry re-echoes from shore to shore
   Of this, our *Christian* land ;
A cry for men to unsheathe the sword,
For the demon of battle is abroad,
   And the spark to a flame is fanned

By those who, by word, and deed, and pen,
Prey on the passions and fears of men,
   And a madness has filled the air—
A madness that thirsts for a brother's life,
A restless fever of war and strife,
   Till we bow 'neath a deep despair ;

For men caress the horrible thing,
And songs of praise in its glory sing,
   And its mighty deeds rehearse,

As though 'twere an angel from heaven that came,
Instead of a devil of sin and shame—
    A blessing, instead of a curse.

War! War! War! War!
As they glibly talk the subject o'er,
    Do they think of what it means?
Do they think of the heaps of mangled slain
Bestrewing the horrible battle plain,
    Of the ghastly, terrible scenes?—

Of the dying soldiers' pitiful cry
For help, when no human help is nigh?—
    And, mixed with the cannon's roar,
The groan of the dying, the barbarous yell,
The things that make up that earthly hell,
    The *glorious* field of war?—

Of the widow and children, whose piteous moan
Rises aloft from their cold hearth-stone;
    Of the mother who mourns her boy;
Of the maiden, who weeps for a lover slain,
The touch of whose hand shall never again
    Thrill her whole soul with joy?

Of the houseless, hungry, suffering band
In every city throughout the land,
   Crying in vain for food,
While wealth and treasure—a costly price—
Are offered up as a sacrifice
   On the cruel altar of blood?

War ! War ! War ! War !
Treading in footsteps steeped in gore,
   Bringing famine and misery ;
Lighting the earth with a lurid flame,
And making even Christ's holy name
   But a ghastly mockery.

Would that we all who profess that name
Would ponder well on the sin and shame,
   On the terrible guilt, before,
With a false desire and selfish aim,
And a feverish thirst for that thing called fame,
   We plunge in the sea of war.

PEACE.

COME, holy Peace, enrobed in spotless white!
Speak to the nations words of heavenly might;
    Bid carnage cease,
And o'er the tumult spread thy wings of light:
    Come, holy peace!

Thy thankless children spurned thy fond embrace,
And set the demon battle in thy place;
    Now our sad eyes
Would fain behold once more thy smiling face:
    Bright Peace, arise!

Come, holy Peace! begin thy glorious reign;
Banish the battle's tumult, strife and pain:
    Come, spirit blest,
Gather mankind beneath thy wings again,
    And give us rest.

THE DYING SOLDIER.

THE day was done, the fatal field was fought;
Upon the ground a thousand manly hearts
Lay still and cold, ambition's sacrifice.
But men applauding praised the fearful work,
And said it was a glorious victory.

Upon a bleak and barren crag of rock,
Around whose base a foaming torrent roared,
A rough rude hovel stood alone; and there
A wounded soldier, who had fallen near,
Had crept for shelter from the noon-tide rays;
And there, when the dread fight was o'er, he lay
And watched the red sun sinking in the west,
And lighting with a lurid glow the plain
Already with a deeper colour tinged.
Pain racked his limbs, and parchèd were his lips,
And dry with thirst; but there was no one near
To bind his wounds, or give him of the stream

That freely flowed before his eager eyes,
So near, and yet so deep below his reach;
And fast the shadows deepened, and the clouds
Rose on the far horizon, and the wind
Around the wretched hut blew cold and chill,
And swept across the desolated scene
With a sad sigh, and moaned above the dead,
Like friends and kindred mourning for their loss.
And soon dense darkness reigned supreme; and then
Came on the air the loud and sullen roll
Of distant thunder. Loud and louder grew
The sound, as nearer still the tempest came;
And then, in maddened fury fell the rain,
And fierce and bright the vivid lightning gleamed,
And, fearful to behold, each flash revealed
The battle plain, where, stiff, and stark, and cold,
The dead men lay, with faces upward turned
Unto the heavens; and, as o'er them passed
The lightning's flash, a shudder seemed to run
Across their features, and the wounded man
In horror closed his eyes upon the sight.
But still a dreadful fascination held
His mind and he was fain to look again.
And now across his fevered brain there crept

A dreadful vision; for he thought he saw
Passing above the dead two phantom hosts,
Who on each other warred; a fearful strife ;
And in each flash of lightning he beheld
The cannon's gleam, and in the thunder's roar
He heard the boom of the artillery,
And saw the deadly shot skim o'er the field,
Mowing down men and horses in its course,
As grass before the scythe.   Then on the wind
Came the sharp trumpet blast, and he beheld
A troop of horsemen, with their lances couched,
Who swiftly bore towards him where he lay;
And as he raised his arm, and cried aloud,
A sharp and sudden pain shot through his limbs,
And madly whirled his brain, and then there came
Across his fevered soul a solemn lull.

And now the storm rolled fitfully away,
As yielding to the solemn calm that stole
Across his mind, he fell asleep and dreamed.
And in his dreams, once more he saw his home,
The quiet grey farmhouse amidst the fields,
The garden, and the orchard rich with fruit;
The peaceful river, and the village spire

Pointing aloft from its surrounding trees;
And then, at the soft eventide he walked
And held sweet converse with the one he loved,
And pressed her hand, and spoke of joys to come;
While o'er the scene, the sunlight's golden glow
In mellow sweetness shone, and on his ear
The soft-toned cadence of the village bells
Stole in sweet harmony. Across the scene
The evening shadows fell, and lowing herds
Wound homeward from the pastures, and the birds
From the green trees poured forth their even-song.
Then backward flew his vision, and once more
A boy he roamed, with playmates wild and free,
And all day long the green and shady woods
Resounded with their laughter and their songs.
Then backward, backward, still the vision passed;
A little child he played about his home;
In the old house from room to room he ran,
Or in the garden chased the butterfly,
And then at close of day he knelt beside
His mother's knee, while she with loving words
Taught his young heart to pray; and, as he spake
The simple prayer, he softly sank to rest.
Slowly the night wore on, until at length

Day dawned, and in the early morning light
They found him in the hovel rough and rude,
With stiffened limbs, his hands still clasped in prayer.

Upon the field the morning sunlight gleamed,
Upon a thousand corpses lying there;
But men, applauding, praised the ghastly work,
And said it was a glorious victory.

CHRISTMAS, 1878.

"And laid him in a manger; because there was no room for them in the inn."

No room, oh, mother! 'midst the busy throng
Within, for thee to lay thy new-born child:
Not unto him, the holy one, belong
Comfort and rest and ease; the night wind wild
Pierces the lowly roof beneath whose shade,
On humble couch the child of God is laid.

No room,—Lord Christ! as in the days of old,
So now the busy world doth pass thee by;
Fierce wars still rage, and avarice and gold
Hold sway; and our vain faithless hearts outcry,
In all their stubborn selfishness and sin,
"No room for thee, oh, holy babe, within."

No room,—oh, prince of peace ! we sing thy praise,
And hail the glory of thy holy birth ;
Again with loud accord our voices raise
The angels' hymn of " Peace, good will on earth ; "
While on the breeze, repeated o'er and o'er,
Comes mingling with the strain the battle's roar.

No room,—for over hill and vale are heard
The tramp of armies and the clang of arms ;
Instead of thy pure gospel's peaceful word,
The cannon's thunder with its wild alarms ;
And burning villages, and blood-stained plains,
Show where the fiend of war triumphant reigns.

No room for thee—amid the angry strife,
Ambition's aim, pride's false desire ; but still
Though dreary be the darksome night of life,
And overhead the wild winds whistle shrill,
Thou liest cradled in the loving breast,
That like to Bethlehem's manger gives thee rest.

A CHRISTMAS LEGEND.

'TWAS on a Christmas Eve, long years ago,
The frost was keen, the country white with snow,
With dreary sound, the melancholy breeze
Sighed through the branches of the leafless trees,
The sun with stormy face sank to his rest,
Lighting with crimson glare the distant west,
The twilight shadows gathered o'er the sky,
And with loud wail, the wintry wind rose high,
The darkness deepened fast, and over all
The silent, feathery snow began to fall.
A woman, wending on her homeward way
Unto a neighbouring town, at close of day,
In crossing a wide waste of moor and fen,
Mistook the path that she should go; and when
Night's darkness spread around, it found her still
Afar from home, with weary feet, and chill
And sinking 'neath the cold; nor knew which way,
Amid the gathering gloom, the city lay.

Peering into the darkness of the night,
To gain perchance some welcome ray of light,
Some well-known thing her frighted heart to cheer,
And tell her that the path she sought was near,
Long hours she wandered o'er the lonely plain,
And sought to find her homeward way in vain;
While round her path the blinding snow fell fast,
And swept in driving clouds before the blast.
With fearful heart, she raised her voice on high,
And cried aloud for help; but no reply
Came back, except the night winds dismal wail.
Again she cried; until, upon the gale,
At length she heard an answering voice that said,
" Courage, faint heart, I come, be not afraid."
A mighty blast swept by with fury wild;
And in the hush that followed it, a child
In peasant garb she saw before her stand,
Bearing a lighted lantern in his hand.
A boy of beauty, wondrous fair to see,
Who said unto the woman, " Follow me."
And wondering, she followed through the night;
The boy went on before her, and the light
He carried, shed its lustrous rays around,
And brightly glistened on the snow-clad ground.

And sparkled on long icicles that hung
From leafless trees, to which the ivy clung,
Like memory to the belovèd dead;
Then shone on holly bush, with berries red,
On ice-bound dyke, and gnarled trunk, that lay,
Fallen from pride, and rotting by the way;
Objects that flashed a moment on the sight,
And then were swallowed up again in night.
At length, the gloomy darkness studding o'er,
The welcome lights shone on the river shore;
And soon they reached the margin of the flood,
Upon whose farther bank the city stood;
Then, crossed the long stone bridge, and then their feet
Trod through the silence of the snow-clad street.
And still before her face the boy went on,
By many a dwelling where the warm light shone
From casements where the laugh and merry din
Of song and dance, told of the mirth within.
Through the deserted streets he led the way,
Unto the quarter where her dwelling lay;
Then, from a neighbouring steeple, loud and clear,
The chimes proclaimed the morning hour was near;
And rose the distant cadence, soft and sweet,
Of carol singers passing on the street,

Singing the glad song of the Saviour's birth;
" All glory be to God, and peace on earth."
And, as she neared her dwelling, nearer drew
The singers and the carol louder grew.
She paused to listen; for she thought the strain
Was taken up, and echoed back again,
By angel voices, loud, and louder still,
" Glory to God ; on earth, peace and good will."
And then, in wonder great, she turned to where
Her child-guide stood. His face so wondrous fair,
Surpassing all earth's children ; so divine
And gentle was his look, while bright did shine
His lantern's light, and radiant glory shed;
She hid her face, and meekly bowed her head;
For now she knew him—she had reached her door,
Led by the Christ, who had passed on before.

THE OAK AND THE IVY.

THE bright sun shone. Upon the morning breeze
An Oak-tree waved his branches to the sky,
And called aloud : "Of all the forest trees,
Who is so strong and brave of heart as I ?"
The tender Ivy, at his gladsome cry,
Crept softly from her forest-hiding place,
Raised joyously her loving arms on high,
And looking up, with brightly smiling face,
Close clasped her giant lord within her fond embrace.

With darksome clouds the sky was overcast.
The stormy wind arose ; with angry sound
Throughout the forest swept the bitter blast,
Spreading destruction and dismay around :
The mighty monarch low upon the ground
Was laid, with shattered form and broken will ;
But round him yet her arms the Ivy wound,
To shield her lord from every passing ill,
And ever faithful loved the vanquished hero still.

CAST ON THE WATERS.

An aged pine, all weather-worn and sere,
That stood alone a mountain stream beside,
Shed on the flood the last cone of the year,
Then yielded to the wintry storm, and died.
Borne downward by the torrent's foaming tide,
The cone at length on fertile ground was cast,
Where from its seed arose and multiplied,
Tall stately trees whose arms defied the blast,
The founders of a forest, mighty, deep, and vast.

Alone and sad, beneath a cold world's frown,
Within his study sat a hoary sage;
With weary trembling hand he noted down
The last thought of his mind, then closed the page,
Sank 'neath the scorn of an ungrateful age
And died unwept. The thought cast forth with tears
Upon life's flood, grew and defied the rage
Of storm and tempest, banished doubts and fears,
And flourished hale and strong, the hope of after-years.

THE TWO STREAMLETS.

FROM out their distant homes among the hills,
Where purple heather and blue harebells grow,
With rippling murmuring voice two mountain rills
Come down; and sparkling in the golden glow
Of morn, and making music as they go,
With gladsome song their merry way they take,
Now through a rough and rugged course, now flow,
Beside some shady knoll or woodland brake,
Where birds of sweetest song their melodies awake.

Now through the open plain they wend their ways,
'Midst fragrant flowers, and meadows fresh and green,
Now glancing in the noon-tide's sultry rays,
Now sheltered deep their ferny banks between,
Still ever onward flows their silvery sheen,
By forest, fen, and field; and now more wide
Do their converging currents grow, till e'en
Each unto each their murmuring waters glide,
And mingling, onward flow together in one tide.

With merry song, in childhood's early hours,
By varying ways two human beings move,
'Midst sweet melodious birds, and fragrant flowers,
Through sunlit meadow, or through shady grove,
And broader still their onward course doth prove
As nearer yet the murmuring currents roll,
Until they meet in one broad stream of love,
And mingle their full stream of heart and soul,
And flow together on, unto their distant goal.

THE OLD CARILLON.

In their belfry old and grey
    The sweet chimes play,
High above the busy street,
With its tumult and its noise,
    Its cares and joys,
And the rush of passing feet.

He who placed them there of old
    Hath long lain cold,
Many years have passed away,
Since that day when first they rang
    With joyous clang,
Their sweet, simple roundelay.

High above the crowd they ring
  And quaintly sing,
While the tide of time doth flow;
Sing the half-forgotten lays
  Of bye-gone days,
Sing with voices soft and low.

Sing in sweet harmonious chime
  Of vanished time,
Shade and sunshine, smiles and tears,
Sing of many a loving breast
  Long laid to rest,
With its hopes, its joys and fears.

But the busy surging throng
  Heed not the song,
As they pass upon their way
In pursuit of joy or gain;
  The bells' sweet strain
Unto them doth nothing say.

Only to the listening ear
   Their voices clear,
Solemn thoughts and memories bring ;
As on the responsive soul
   The soft tones roll,
This the burden that they sing :—

" There is found a place of rest
   Within the breast,
Where past joys still reign, and o'er
All the tumult and the strife
   And toil of life,
Make sweet music evermore."

From their belfry old and grey
   The sweet chimes say,—
" Listen, listen, to our rhyme,
Happy, oh, thrice happy he
   Whose joys shall be,
Music meet for after-time."

THE EDDYSTONE LIGHTHOUSE.

FOR six score years alone hath he withstood
The tempests' might. Oft times about his base,
With angry roar hath raged the foaming flood,
Dashing its salt spray up into his face ;
Around his head the wild winds held their chase ;
But though full fierce the storm and dark the night,
It ever found him ready at his place,
Upholding o'er the foam a beacon bright,
To guide the wave-toss'd sailor with its welcome light.

But now at length the day is drawing near,
When into other hands he must resign
The charge he holds. Yet ever bright and clear,
Across the seething main the light shall shine,
Guiding the wanderer with its beams benign ;
For still, though his proud days of might are o'er,
Another, fashioned on the same design,
Shall bear aloft the burden that he bore,
And tell of what he was, when he shall be no more.

A WREATH OF SMOKE.

WITH peaceful glow the summer sun shines brightly,
　On laughing rivulet and meadows green,
And the soft murmuring breeze of morning lightly
　Blows, with refreshing breath across the scene.

With lightsome, happy face, each wayside flower
　Looks upward to the clear and azure sky;
The thrush sings sweetly from her shady bower,
　The lark pours forth his gladsome song on high.

From 'midst the trees the church spire tall and slender,
　And red-roofed homesteads of the village glow;
Bathed in the glorious sunlight's golden splendour,
　Through beds of reeds the silent stream doth flow.

Upon the hill, with steady motion turning,
　The sails of the old mill move in the breeze,
Down in the vale a smouldering fire is burning,
　Amidst a dark and sombre mass of trees.

With the soft beauty of the landscape blending,
　A light and curling wreath of smoke doth rise,
And from the dark and shadowy mass ascending,
　Floats upward, on light wing, towards the skies.

In graceful curl its feathery form uplifting,
   It higher soars, and vanishes from view;
Soon shall it join the fleecy vapours drifting
   In fair white clouds across the ethereal blue.

There shall it float with calm majestic motion,
   O'er marsh and moorland, mountain, vale, and plain,
O'er town and village, river, lake, and ocean,
   Until it falls in soft refreshing rain.

So, like the white fantastic smoke enwreathèd,
   Wafted upon the pinions of the wind,
Is every vapourous thought and fancy breathèd
   From out the smouldering embers of the mind.

Cast forth upon the breeze, its course it wendeth
   Obedient to the wayward wind's control;
But not in vain, if from the mist descendeth
   One drop of rain on some responsive soul.

THE END.

www.ingramcontent.com/pod-product-compliance
Lightning Source LLC
Chambersburg PA
CBHW030906260626
47169CB00008B/2709